A SMALL PUDDING for WEE GOWRIE

and other stories of underground creatures

William Mayne

M

MACMILLAN CHILDREN'S BOOKS

LONDON

Illustrated by Martin Cottam

First published 1983 by
MACMILLAN CHILDREN'S BOOKS
A division of Macmillan Publishers Limited
London and Basingstoke

Associated companies throughout the world

Filmset in Optima by Filmtype Services Limited,
Scarborough, North Yorkshire

Printed in Hong Kong

Designed by Sue Williams

ISBN 0-333 34080 9

Contents

Wee Gowrie

A boy called Mungo, and his sister Kirstie, went for a walk one day.

"Just go to the sweetie shop beside the beach, and then come back," their mother said.

"That's all we'll do," said Kirstie. "He's bigger than me, but that's all we'll do, you see."

Boys don't do what their sisters say – but we'll see, we'll see.

They both went down to the sweetie shop. "I've spent my silver penny," said Kirstie, because she was very small. But Mungo knew what money was, until he'd spent it all.

Then they looked at the shining sand, and the sea came rolling in.

"We'll walk down to the edge of it," said Mungo, "we won't go far from land."

They went down on the beach a way, and watched the foamy waves.

"We should go back," said Kirstie. "Mungo, that we must."

"A wee while longer," said Mungo, "and then we'll leave, and go the long way back."

"We've sweeties to eat, we'll not be hungry," said Kirstie. "I suppose it will be all right."

"Of course it will," said Mungo. "We'll go up the cliff on the path." If you don't do what they say sisters begin to cry. Kirstie sniffed, and said that would do, and didn't drop a tear. Mungo thought she was very brave, and told her what he had heard about a giant who lived on the cliffs with his wife in a secret cave.

"In the olden days he ate people up," said Mungo, "when they came too near."

"I do not like that story," said Kirstie. "It's not what I want to hear."

"The story is fine," said Mungo. "It is the giant himself we should worry about."

"Well," said Kirstie, "I don't believe in him."

"His name is Wee Gowrie," said Mungo.

"Then he doesn't sound so bad," said Kirstie. "But let's be going home."

They went up the path on the cliff. Halfway up there was a seat where people came to sit and see the view.

'We'll wait here a bit," said Kirstie. "I'm not out of breath. I'm very strong. I'm never out of breath. But I want a sweetie from the bag. I've finished what I had."

"Then get it quick," said Mungo. Now he wished he had not told the story of Wee Gowrie on the cliff, in case he met him. "Don't be long."

"I'll have one of these," said Kirstie, and she brought out an aniseed ball, large and round, shiny reddish-brown.

Halfway to her mouth it tumbled down, rolled across the path, fell off the cliff, and was lost upon the ground.

"Mungo, Mungo, what shall I do?" she said. "It's gone. It's running down the cliff."

"Well now," said Mungo, who had been watching it. "It's not gone far. I'll clamber down a little way. I see it by that thistle on the slope. It will be easy to get, I hope."

So he slipped under the fence, and climbed down the sloping cliff. Not far away the aniseed ball lay on a leaf, looking very clean.

"This is an adventure for us both," said Mungo, wondering where to put his foot, and what to hold with his hand.

"Are you still there?" said Kirstie, leaning down to look.

"I'm here," said Mungo. "And I'm on my way."

Kirstie waited. She saw the sweetie lying there, but Mungo was out of sight.

"Are you there?" she said. "Are you still all right?"

It seemed that Mungo was busy, because there was no reply.

"Mungo," said Kirstie, crossly, "are you doing nothing? Why don't you reply?"

But Mungo was saying nothing.

"I'll have to have a look," said Kirstie. "I expect the naughty boy has fallen off. But I did not hear a splash or shout. Well, if he hasn't fallen in, perhaps he's fallen out."

She went through the fence to look, and her head was over the edge.

The aniseed ball was there. She wanted that. But Mungo was not. And she wanted him as well.

She turned herself about until her legs began to climb. She was going down for herself. "I'll bring them both along," she said.

Now Mungo, when he was a little down the cliff, found he was on a path. "I'll go along it," he said, "I'll go a little way, that can't be wrong."

He went along, and round a corner of the cliff. A path goes somewhere, always, or it would not be there. This one knew the rule, and led to the mouth of a cave.

Mungo did not think of stories, giants did not come to mind. He forgot Wee Gowrie and went in to look around.

It was not quite dark. Light came in from the sea.

"This is grand fun," thought Mungo. "But now I shall go back."

But when he turned to go Wee Gowrie put out a hand as big as a gate and dragged him in, stood him on a table, and looked at him. Mungo looked at Wee Gowrie, and it was an ugly thing.

"Wife," said Wee Gowrie, "we have company."

"Well, Gowrie, comb your hair," said Wee Gowrie's wife.

"There's such a thing as table manners, lad."

"Bring a dish of turnips my guest and I can share," said Wee Gowrie. He had a voice like rolling tides and rocks grinding under the sea.

"I must be off," said Mungo. "They're wanting me at home."

"I want you much more here," said Wee Gowrie. "Isn't he a bonny guest, wife?"

"Bonnier than you," said Wee Gowrie's wife. "Gowrie, brush your beard."

"Away with fussiness," said Wee Gowrie. "We'll both be as we are, isn't that so, my lad?"

"They're expecting me at home," said Mungo. "I must go."

"I did not expect you at all," said Wee Gowrie. "So you must stay. They've had you plenty, I dare say."

"And there's my little sister," said Mungo. "Not far away."

"There's a welcome for her too," said Wee Gowrie. "Any day. Wee girls are made of meat."

Gowrie's wife brought in a bowl of steaming turnip mash. She put it on the table between them

both. Wee Gowrie put his fingers in and began to eat.

"Reach too, and eat your share, young man," said Wee Gowrie.

"I don't like turnip very well," said Mungo, and "Thank you," he politely said.

"It's all there is," said Wee Gowrie. "And it's fattening and good."

"That's so," said Gowrie's wife. "Gowrie, wipe your chin."

"Turnips don't notice manners," said Gowrie. "Wife, bring another dish."

"That's all there is, Gowrie, pick your teeth," said his wife.

"Bring another dish for the bones," said Wee Gowrie.

"Aye, that," said Gowrie's wife. "Another dish for the bones."

"But," said Mungo, "there are no bones in turnips."

"Well, that is so," said Gowrie. "But I know where there are some bones, lad." And his great hand picked Mungo up and held him in front of the great beard, and in front of the great chin, and in front of the great teeth.

Gowrie's wife brought in an empty dish for the bones.

Now Kirstie had had a great deal of trouble on the cliff. Her legs were not long enough to reach, and when they did, her skirt caught on a thorn, and when she had got free she found it torn, and landed on her bottom.

She did not cry at all because somehow on the way she found the aniseed ball.

For now she put it in the bag, and climbed the cliff again.

She came to the little path that Mungo found, and wondered if he might have gone that way, and walked that track and not come back.

Kirstie walked that way. She was very frightened all the time. She remembered the giant Wee Gowrie. She knew he lived on the cliff. Mungo had told her the story, and she knew that if . . .

She knew that if Wee Gowrie was there, and Mungo got too near, Wee Gowrie would eat him up, and there was no one about to hear.

So when she came to the cave she knew at once what it was. She knew Wee Gowrie was in it, and Mungo was there as well. She knew that Wee Gowrie's wife was ready and waiting with another large dish for the bones.

"Well, I will go instead," said Kirstie. "He went to rescue my aniseed ball, so I'll do something for him. I hope Wee Gowrie does not mind my skirt is torn, my knees are scratched, and I'm sure my bottom's muddy."

When she stood inside the cave, and heard Wee Gowrie laugh, she thought she should go home at once, before it was too late. And then she bravely thought she would go further in, watch a while, and wait.

In she went, and there she saw Mungo, and Wee

Gowrie, and his wife. And there were dishes and plates and knives and forks, and Wee Gowrie was horribly fat, and so was his wife.

Mungo was terribly thin and small and about to lose his life.

"Is that Wee Gowrie?" said Kirstie. "It is I believe. Aren't you thirsty? Would you not like a drink?" She saw he was the sort to take a drink with both his ugly hands.

"I would," said Wee Gowrie. "Turnip is dreadfully dry. Wife get me a barrel of ale, my throat is dusty."

"I'll bring you a bowl of water," said his wife, "and Gowrie, wash behind your ears!"

Wee Gowrie drank, and that was fine, but he held Mungo still. Kirstie stood by the door and thought she did not care to be eaten by anyone so rough.

14

"Wife, bring me a knife," said Wee Gowrie. "I'll have a slice of boy."

"Here's a knife," said Gowrie's wife. "And Gowrie, cut your nails."

"Don't vex me," said Wee Gowrie. "Or next I'll make you cook you."

Kirstie came in and tapped Wee Gowrie on the knee. "Wee Gowrie, have your pudding first," she said, "and Mungo last of all." And she held up a sweetie for him, the biggest aniseed ball.

"Well now, what's this?" Wee Gowrie said. "Your pudding is not so big, but it's sweet and tastes very good. Give me the rest and your brother's next, and you'll be last and best."

But Kirstie took herself away across the floor and near the door and Wee Gowrie had to follow.

"Wee Gowrie has to crawl," said Kirstie, "if he wants an aniseed ball."

And Wee Gowrie had to crawl.

"What's this?" said his wife. "Is it Gowrie, sweep the floor?"

"It's Gowrie, come for pudding," said Kirstie. "Gowrie, use both hands."

"I'll catch you both," Wee Gowrie said. "One each for my wife and me."

An aniseed ball rolled down the hall, along the floor, out of the door.

To chase it well Wee Gowrie put Mungo down, and on all fours he fell. "Not since I was a wee lad with my marbles did I crawl," he said.

But Mungo did not listen. Mungo ran. Kirstie ran with him.

Just behind them hobbled Wee Gowrie, much bigger than them both.

"We'll not get far," said Mungo.

"I think we will," said Kirstie. "Look."

They looked round, and there was Wee Gowrie, fast in his front door, too stout to get out; or the door was so thin it kept him in. Back or forth, up or down, side to side, he could not move.

"On your knees?" said his wife. "Gowrie, say your prayers."

"I'm sorry for him," said Mungo. "Eating turnip all the time."

"I pity him," said Kirstie, "with not many manners and not much pudding," and she rolled him another aniseed ball. She said, "That's all."

But it was not all. When they got home Mungo and his sister Kirstie told the tale. The people of the town came out. They knew the story of wicked Wee Gowrie was true, and were glad to see him stuck so firm where he could do no harm.

They were kind to him. He had eaten no one that they knew, only sailors in the olden time. They lit a little fire to keep him warm, and when he was thin enough they let him out. They combed his hair and brushed his beard and gave him new trousers to wear, because his had holes in the knee.

They gave him a house by the sea, and a job of work to do. He keeps the bowling green, and can often be seen crawling across the grass, hoping he'll catch up with a great big aniseed ball. Kirstie goes down now and then and takes him a bag of sweeties for a treat, and gives him some of them, not all.

And he knows that eating people is wrong and a thing he should not do, but now and then he might, if their parents ask him right, nibble a naughty child or two.

When the Swamp dried up

There was a boy called Garun Hamilton, who was nearly lost for ever. And it was not his fault. No one knows whose fault it was, except that person, and he won't say.

Garun was with his parents, his brother and his sister, waiting at the Museum Station of Melbourne underground railway, called the Metro, when something came along the tracks that was not a train.

No. It was Bunyip. He came shuffling and hopping along, in his great white skin and the gingery long fur that is not quite hair and is not quite feathers, but something in between: if you get near, look, and you will see the hairs have branches.

19

He came along on his marshy feet, exploring the tunnel. He was upright and huge. He breathed snortingly, because he had flaps over his nostrils to keep out water.

He smelt of bubbly, muddy, greenish swamp. It is how he is. After all, man smells worst of anything to most other animals.

The people on the platform stopped their talk. "Just look at that," was all they said, and then were quiet, and watched Bunyip going on his way. He did not look at them. Perhaps he did not like their smell.

Flop, flop, went his feet. The people on the platform kept quite still and wished their train would come and take them all straight home.

But next to Garun stood a naughty boy, the naughty boy whose name we do not know. The boy had in his pocket a gum nut, the hard fruit of the eucalyptus tree. He had kept it in case it became useful. And now it did, but not in any wise manner.

The boy took the gum nut from his pocket, bent his elbow, took good aim, and threw it at Bunyip. The gum nut hit Bunyip on the side of the head.

Bunyip stopped his walk, and turned, and looked. A hundred faces turned and looked at him.

Bunyip put out a long and hairy/feathery arm. He picked up Garun, tucked him under the long and hairy/feathery arm, and walked on into the tunnel with him. Both disappeared into the darkness.

Garun was very interested in what was happening, but somehow did not have enough breath to say so. On the platform Mr and Mrs Hamilton, and the two children, had leapt forward with a shout and cry. But they were too late, because at once a train drew in and filled the entrance to the tunnel.

Mr Hamilton said to the driver, "Stop."

The driver said, "I have, mate, or you wouldn't be stood there talking to me. You'd be running at sixty k.p.h."

"Then don't go any further," said Mr Hamilton. "There's a Bunyip on the track."

"Time you went home and took it easy, mate," said the driver. "That's my green light, and off I go."

But Mrs Hamilton wasted no time on words. She got in the train and pulled the alarm, and it could not go.

Of course there was confusion, and strife, and policemen running in to sort the matter out. So it

was some time before anyone got into the tunnel and followed after Bunyip and his captive.

There was nothing to be seen. Somewhere under the city streets Bunyip had got away.

Metro Tragedy, the *Herald* said that night, **Monster Steals Melbourne Boy.**

Grisly Terror at Museum, said the *Age* next day.

For a time we have to leave the anguished parents, two hungry children, a baffled police force, and an angry Metro manager. We must find out how and why the Bunyip was in that place. The only thing we shall not find is the name of the actual naughty larrikin who threw the gum nut.

Long before this time, before men came to Melbourne, there was a fine swamp at the mouth of the Yarra river. The river went down the middle, and the marshes stretched along either side. In the muddy places, among the wild birds, Bunyip had his home.

He was a monster, but monsters are allowed. He had his family in the marshes, and they were all monsters too. He loved them monstrously. They live a long time, and they take hundreds of years to grow, but they do not worry, because there are no Bunyip schools.

When ships came Bunyip swam to them and winked at the figureheads, but those lovely ladies only smiled and said nothing at all. Bunyip's wife said, "Don't talk to them, Bunyip dear; we don't know who they are."

So Bunyip did not go that way again. He left the ships, ignored the sailors, and lounged about the swamp, still happy.

One day he went up the river and saw a curious thing. There was a bridge, and on the bridge a horse and cart.

"I will not have you talking to the cart," said his wife. "And neither of us believes in horses, I hope."

"Indeed no," said Bunyip. "Quite imaginary."

But men were coming, and horses and carts and cows. And more ships came. Bunyip began to find curious things in the swamp, spoiling the texture and flavour of the mud. Boys came to the water's edge and hung down hooks for fish. Bunyip could catch fish easy. Sometimes he would hang one on a hook, sometimes he would hang a boot, and often eat the bait.

But as time went by, and before the children were

very much older, men had sent more and more ships into the swamp, and built walls round it, and started to dry it up. They built houses on it. Bunyip thought the first house he saw was a stranded ship, and pushed it into the river. He was very much shouted at.

"Do not help them any more, Bunyip," said his wife. "We don't want them helping us. I wonder what sort of a thing they are?"

"We should try one for supper," said Bunyip.

"They don't look very wholesome," said his wife.

There were railways round the swamp, there were factories at the edge, there were roads across, there were lights on long poles. There was a tiresome ferry boat that went through their bedroom twenty times a day. At length there was not enough swamp to live in.

"We could try the Zoo," said Bunyip.

"It costs fifty cents to get in," said his wife. "We don't have money."

Bunyip found some lovely drains. There was not much view, but the mud was good. That was the way Bunyip became an underground creature, exploring in tunnels, and seeing where they went.

There are more tunnels than you hear about, under a city. Bunyip knows them all. If he can't get up there himself he puts along a hairy/feathery arm, and then a fine, feeling finger. Look in the gullies along the street, and see him move his wrist.

"A Metro tunnel's not the best," he said. "Too dry. But good and roomy. I use it for a short cut now and then."

"Don't get talking to the trains," said his wife. She stayed with her children in an outfall by the docks.

This is where we began to hear of Garun Hamilton.

One day Bunyip came home with a bundle.
"Ah," said Mrs Bunyip. "Tea."

"No," said Bunyip. "It's a young one of them, and it threw a stone at me. I thought that if we kept him a little while, say seventy years, we might teach him to be polite."

"I did not do it," said Garun. "I am a conservation freak. It was another boy."

"I'm sure it's so," said Mrs Bunyip. "He looks too good for tricks like that."

"I'm sorry, boy," said Bunyip. "I must have made an error. But stay the night, and I'll take you home tomorrow."

"Look, Mummy," said the little Bunyips, "he hasn't any fur. He must get dreadful dry."

So Garun played Leap-Bunyip with them, and games called Splash and Puddle. Then he leaned against the mother Bunyip while she told a story. He could not understand every word, but it made the babies laugh.

He went to sleep in comfortable mud, with a Bunyip baby either side. Mother Bunyip sang them all to sleep with a gurgling marshy song.

In the morning Bunyip took him home. Garun knew his address, where his house was, the number of his telephone, his postcode, but had no idea which drain to catch to get there.

It took them all the morning. On the surface a whole city was searching for Garun. But under the ground Garun was coming home. Bunyip loved the scenery under there, and so they went the pretty way, by the South Circular Drain and the Elizabeth Street Overpass, which is far below the street, and along the Victoria Street Double Plummet, and the Heidelberg Siphon, where you loop the loop. They crossed the river Yarra in an iron tube.

"I know all the lurks," said Bunyip.

"It's fun," said Garun.

They came along the storm duct under Studley Park.

"You'll have to go up through a grating and take a look around," said Bunyip. "I think we're somewhere near."

"I could get out and walk," said Garun.

"I'll take you home," said Bunyip. "They'd rather know it was all a mistake."

They came out in Kellet Reserve, and walked around the corner, and in at the door of 1/317.

"Two Bunyips," said Mrs Hamilton. "Come for the rest of us, I dare say."

"No," said Garun. "They've been very kind. It was all a mistake, you see."

"I'm sure I'm glad you're home again," said his

mother, "but I'll hug when you've washed. There's something about you called mud."

"I'll be off," said Bunyip. "Now I've brought him home."

"Stay and have a cup of tea," said Mrs Hamilton. "Or do you think a bucketful would suit you better?"

"It's kind of you, but I'd better be going," said Bunyip. "I get sunstroke very easy, out of the water like this. But Garun knows where we live, and ask him to call any time. And if I may I'll bring my youngsters round some day to play with yours. They don't get out very much, because swamps aren't what they were."

"It's very kind," said Mrs Hamilton.

"We'll see you to the drain," said Garun.

So they waved him goodbye by the edge of the road. Then Garun rang up the police and said he was home.

He went to school in the afternoon, but Bunyip babies never go.

Inside the wall

Tifan was a lucky elf, he thought. His house was on the outside of the City Wall, where no Men could see him. Men lived inside the City, but in the wall, and in the ground under it, lived all sorts of creatures, and Tifan was only one of them.

He spent his time doing what he liked best, fishing from his window, which overlooked the moat at the bottom of the wall. He fished in the morning and the evening, and did his cooking and shopping and visiting in the afternoon. Everyone in the wall was happy and busy.

But one morning Tifan woke up and found a noise in his house. Something was jumping sloppily round and round, like a frog in a puddle.

That is a silly thing to think, thought Tifan. Frogs live down in the moat, not up here. He went to see what it really was.

It was a Frog – a large, green, worried Frog, going round Tifan's kitchen in a watery puddle. It jumped from floor to table. It knocked the teapot off, and broke it.

"Too dry," said the Frog, and jumped down into the puddle. "Too wet," he said, and jumped up again. Over went the milk jug and the sugar.

"Too dry," said the Frog. "Oh dear."

"Too much," said Tifan. "Much too much. Stop it, Frog."

"Too dry, too wet," said the Frog, jumping into the sink and on to the cooker.

"This way, Frog," said Tifan, getting round behind it and pushing it out of the kitchen, out past his bed by the window, and on to the window ledge.

"Too high," said the Frog.

"Too bad," said Tifan, and pushed him out.

"Too far," said the Frog, and he fell down the wall and into the water of the moat. Then he swam away.

"And that's that," said Tifan, wiping up a wet footprint in the bedroom, and going to tidy the kitchen.

That wasn't all. In the kitchen a family of Ants was cleaning up the sugar for him. Ants often come in houses and take sugar away. It is how they do their shopping. But these Ants had come to stay. They mumbled to each other. "Send out for Grandma," they said, "and cousin Formy would like this, there's plenty here for everyone. The Queen's coming, so we'll leave a lump for her. Yes, everybody's welcome."

"You are not welcome," shouted Tifan. "That is my sugar and I wish you would go away."

"There's a kind elf," muttered the Ants to each other. They don't say anything loud but they say it all the time. "We hoped you weren't going to be elfish. There's lots more coming. You haven't any cake, have you?"

Tifan did not know what to do with thousands of Ants, swarming over his kitchen. If he was nasty to them they would stop biting the sugar, and bite him instead.

At least, he thought, I'll stop them coming in, because they look as if they are going to stay.

He went to look for some tiny hole.

He found a large one in the bottom of the broom cupboard. The Frog had come up that way. And more Ants were coming up, complaining about the rough floor, bringing their Queen.

"Do be careful," she was saying. "What a clumsy lot you are. And there, I've laid another lovely little egg. What a pretty thing it is, and it has its father's shell, I'm sure. Hold me tight. And look, I've laid another lovely little egg. What a pretty thing it is, and it has its father's shell."

That was all she could say all day.

She began to live on Tifan's pillow. She talked all the time; the other Ants talked all the time; and Tifan could not have breakfast because they had eaten it.

He looked at the hole. A company of Woodlice came up out of it, yawning and groaning. They had come a long way on a hard march. Hundreds of them stretched out on Tifan's floor, turned on their backs, and wriggled their tired feet and legs. The room looked as if it had a moving carpet.

They got up and started eating the wardrobe, which is what they like.

"Stop!" said Tifan, banging the wardrobe door. But nothing stopped them. At least they did not talk as they munched. They left the nails, that was all.

When they had eaten they shouted "Three cheers!" rolled up into little balls, and went to sleep.

Before that, more things had come out of the hole.

There was a troop of Hamster Scouts running together, climbing the curtains, tearing up the counterpane to make a camp, and blowing whistles. "Preep preep," they went, "can you hear me, Patrol Leader?"

"Preep, preep, loud and clear. Over. Over and out."

What am I going to do? thought Tifan. Don't they know it is my house, not theirs?

They didn't. The Woodlice stayed rolled up when he asked them. The Queen of the Ants said she had laid another nice little egg. The Leader of the Hamster Scouts said he had to look after his lads, and couldn't talk to visitors.

Then slow Slow-worm crawled in, tripped over

the Woodlice, went to sleep in the empty teapot and
started snoring.

There came a young Rat, wearing a soldiery hat,
carrying a sword. He knew what he was doing. He
spoke to the Leader of the Hamsters, asking whether
everything was in order.

"Fine," said the Leader. "My lads have set up
camp. We'll have a sing-song, and then we'll sleep
all day. Yes, couldn't be better."

"Good," said the young Rat. He said, "Good
morning, Elf," to Tifan, and went down the hole
again.

I'll block that hole up, thought Tifan. But it was
too late. Up came two Weasels, with pistols hung
on their belts.

"This seems all right," they said. "You can come up," they shouted, looking down the hole again. They went to investigate the larder. Tifan felt hungry, but did not know what there was left to eat.

Up came a band of Stoats, with guns. They began target practice on Tifan's cups. They marched up and down, saluting. They shouted for fried eggs and cups of tea.

Tifan stood in a corner wishing no one else was there, and that he had space for himself, because Ants were crawling on his feet, Woodlice were nibbling his fingernails, Hamster lads were bumping into him with their sticks, Weasels were raiding his refrigerator, and Stoats were shouting orders in his ear.

Tifan could not bear it. He closed his eyes so that he could not see the mess. He covered his ears, so that he could not hear. He opened his mouth to shout "Help!" He sat down on the floor where he was.

Where he sat down there was no floor. He had forgotten. He sat down on the hole; he sat down in the hole; he sat down through the hole; and he went on sitting on nothing until he landed.

He landed on something soft and cushiony. That was lucky. The bottom of a hole is usually harder than the hole itself.

This one was soft. "Ouf," it said. "Ooh-ah."

Tifan had landed on somebody. He got off. He thought it was probably someone going up to his house, to make more noise and muddle, without asking.

It was not that sort of person at all. It was Old Mother Toad. She smiled at him quite nicely. Elves are not very heavy. "You usually come out through your front door," she said. "Not through the floor of the broom cupboard."

"I know," said Tifan. "My visitors usually come

through the front door, too. But today they have come through my broom cupboard, and are eating me out of house and home. Now I have fallen down the hole myself."

"I've had to move house too," said Old Mother Toad.

"Why have you had to move?" asked Tifan.

"Because my house is full of mud and water," said Old Mother Toad. "Your visitors moved for the same reason. Down below, where it begins to be underground, the moat has got into the wall and begun to knock it down."

"Oh, then I am sorry for the poor things," said Tifan.

"They had to climb up the cracks in the wall, so they could not knock. I expect they think you are another flooded-out person."

"I am," said Tifan. "I am flooded out with Hamster Scouts and Ants."

"I've been out in the Men's part of town, to tell them," said Old Mother Toad. "But all I can say is 'Croak' and they don't hear and if they did they wouldn't understand."

"Someone else will have to go," said Tifan.

"You should," said Old Mother Toad. "You can speak their words. You can read their notices. Tell them the wall is falling down and your house is going to fill with mud. Listen. It is coming."

Tifan listened, and he could hear mud rising up in the wall. "I don't mind a little mud," he said. "Everything is spoilt already. I just don't want to go outside."

"But that is the brave and good thing to do, Elf," said Old Mother Toad. "Go and find the Mayor and tell him. Save our lives."

Tifan did what she said. He found his way to the street of Men, and looked out at it from the bottom of a wall.

And I haven't even a hat with me, he said to himself. A polite Elf never goes without a hat.

He stepped out into the street. A dog came up to see whether he was easy to eat. Tifan was not easy to eat. He had a trick against dogs. The trick was to make himself have no smell at all. The dog did not understand that, and went away, worrying about his nose.

A cat came stepping up, seeing Tifan go by like a little shadow. Tifan pulled her whiskers, and she went back to her window to watch something else.

The front wheel of a bicycle went one side of him, the back wheel the other, and he was nearly run over.

A horse and cart came trampling close to him.

People blinked at him and wiped their glasses clean, thinking he was a mark.

He was not a mark. He was Tifan the Elf, hurrying to the Mayor in the middle of the town. He hated the noise and the bright lights and the crowds, and the long straight streets. And when you are small and close to the ground you find out just how dirty the streets are.

He went on, though rain began to fall and the gutters filled with water. He had to swim, and struggle through mud.

He went on, though rubbish was thrown on him. No Elf likes to be knocked over by an old cabbage leaf. He does not think it at all funny.

He climbed the steps of the Town Hall, each one as high as himself. At the top was a great door that he could not open. He banged on it with his hands, but made no sound. He kicked it, and no Man heard. But the old Dormouse who watched the building by night woke from a dream and saw Tifan waiting. He let him in through a dormousy door, and told him where to find the Mayor.

"I shall tell him everything," said Tifan. "About the Hamster Scouts, the Ants, the Slow-worm in the teapot; all those things."

When he began the story of the Frog the Mayor stopped him and said, "First tell me where you live, because my Men will go to put the matter right. Our City Wall is very important."

Tifan told the Mayor his address. The Mayor told his Men.

Tifan told his story about who had come into his house, and what they said and did. The Mayor shook his head, said "How sad," and gave him a cup of tea.

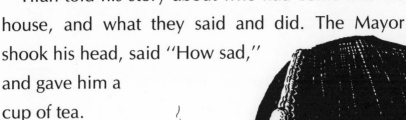

Then Tifan hurried home. The streets were dangerous with children running home from school, and prams parading up and down.

The worst thing of all had happened while he was away. The Mayor's Men had pulled a length of city wall right down and taken it away. And in that piece of wall was Tifan's house.

"What shall I do?" he said, "my home has gone." He sat down on a nearby stone, and felt miserable.

The stone he sat on gave a sigh. "Ouf," it said, "Ooh-ah." It was Old Mother Toad again. "I waited for you," she said, "and here you are."

"I told them what the trouble was," said Tifan. "And they pulled my house quite down."

"Well, yes," said Old Mother Toad. "They would. They'd have to. They'll put it up again in time. But now we've gone to live under the trees in the Park. Come and see. It's not so bad."

Tifan went with her. First they met the Ants.

"We've cleared the ground and made it smooth," they said. "We did it for you and our Queen. And we've sent for our cousin Formy and the others."

They met the hundreds of Woodlice, who had eaten all day and chewed out caves in the trees where people could live.

"Preep, preep," went the whistle of the Hamster Scouts. They were fully trained by now, and cooking stew. Slow Slow-worm had come out through the teapot spout, and laid himself in a row to be sat on beside the camp fire. Chief cook was the young Rat, and chief huntsmen were the two Weasels with pistols. They had shot a parsnip dead for the stew.

To guard them all the band of Stoats, with their guns, marched up and down, saluting, and having second helpings of fried eggs, and cups of tea.

They all said how brave Tifan had been to go through the dangers of the town to tell the Mayor of their mud and flood. Tifan blushed, and the Woodlice gave three cheers.

After that they went to sleep. In a week or two the Men had finished all the work. Tifan went down to see his house, and there it was again, just as it used to be. On the wall a picture hung, of Tifan himself, and under it the words said: *Tifan, a brave elf, who went through many dangers to save his neighbours.*

Tifan was pleased at that, pleased to be at home. But now and then he wakes and thinks it is too quiet, though he doesn't really want a Frog to jump alarmingly around his kitchen, too wet, too dry, breaking the teapot, and all that happens after that.

Nebuchendrie

In the middle of the story a Prince comes riding over the mountains.

But at the beginning there was a little Princess, not old enough to choose herself a name.

Her father was King and chief, and kept a thousand cows and a thousand sheep. Her mother kept a thousand fields of corn and a thousand melon gardens.

They were both busy early in the morning and late at night, so they hired a woman to look after the Princess when they were out.

The woman was called Rianch.

"She is not pretty to look at," said the Queen.

"That does not matter," said the King. "Beside my daughter and my wife, everyone is plain."

"She is very strict," said the Queen.

"Nothing can replace a mother," said the King.

And they left their little daughter day after day with Rianch, who was not beautiful, and who was strict.

As the days went by she became even less beautiful and even more strict.

"I do not like her all the time," said the little Princess.

"My dear, and my dear," said the Queen.

"You would say the same of your own mother," said the King. "Now and then, I'm sure."

"The Princess must know who is in charge," said Rianch. "May it please your Royal Chief Highnesses."

Days went by again, and it was certain that Rianch became ugly and severe. But the little Princess thought that she herself must be wicked and wrong, and grew sad.

At night she was asleep before the King and

Queen came back, and in the morning she woke when they had left.

"I shall tell them tomorrow," she told Rianch. But when she saw Rianch coming she ran into the yard and climbed a tree, where Rianch could not follow.

"I shall wait," said Rianch. "We'll see who is master here. And you shall have what you ask for."

"I do not want anything," said the Princess. And the sun came up and was hot on her head. "My head aches," she said.

"So let the sun give pain," said Rianch. And the Princess had a headache as hot as the sun itself.

She grew hungry. "I should like to eat," she said. "Maize and melons and soft cheese."

"You shall hunger," said Rianch. "You shall."

The Princess grew thirsty.

"I should like to drink," she said, "I am dry."

"And you shall stay dry," said Rianch. "You shall thirst. Now I shall go away and wait for you. I am the master now. There is nothing you can do about that." And she went away. "I name you Nebuchendrie," she said. "Nebuchendrie."

In the words of that country it means the hungry and thirsty one living under the ground.

After a long time the little Princess came down from the tree. Her head hurt, she was weak from hunger, and her tongue lay in her mouth like a cinder.

She went to the well in the courtyard for a drink of water, and to cool her head. What happened there we do not know. But when the King and Queen came back from their flocks and gardens the Princess could not be found, and Rianch had been seen running back to her own village.

The King and Queen sent for Rianch, but she did not come. The whole land was searched, but Rianch and the Princess seemed lost.

The King and Queen, full of sorrow, went back to their thousands of duties, because at that time of year water was hard to get, and many cows and sheep, many fields and gardens, need a great deal of water.

There came the rains. Rivers and lakes, tanks and cisterns, filled up; and water to spare ran into the ground to fill the wells. There was less hard work to be done. The King and Queen sat in their hut, thought sad thoughts, and wished they heard their daughter's little voice.

Then the rains were over, the sky was clear of clouds, and the King and Queen sat in the court-yard. They saw that the well was drying up, the water low when it should be high. They sent a man down to find what was wrong, but the man did not come up. He called out, "Nebuchendrie." That was all.

And people came from village and town to say their wells were drying too.

"There is water in the lakes," said the King.

"There is water in the tanks and cisterns," said the Queen.

But there was not water in those places for long. When it was used up the thousand cows and the thousand sheep drank of the sea and died; the thousand fields turned to dust; the melon gardens dried to tinder and took fire, and there was nothing left.

"All the bad things of the world have happened to us," said the King. He and the Queen, and the people, lived on drops of water, few grains of corn, and some leaves, until the coming of the rains again.

Then the rivers and lakes, the tanks and cisterns, filled, and water flowed; but the wells stayed dry.

A worse thing happened. By night there came a black hungry thing out of the wells, a thing like a serpent, that would catch and eat people, cows, horses, dogs, children. This thing was called Nebuchendrie. No one knew who named it Nebuchendrie, but we know Rianch did so.

It was the same for year after year. A little old woman from one of the villages said to the King, "And who is master now? Nebuchendrie?"

"I am," said the King. "Nebuchendrie is not. I am chief, king and master."

"Then tell us what to do," said the Queen, and all the people. "One more year of drought and we shall all be dead."

"This is what we do," said the King, "and there is nothing else. We shall line up two and two, men, women, children, and march across the mountains to the next kingdom, and there we shall sell ourselves as slaves. Or we stay here and die."

So the people lined up and crossed the mountains. First the heat was great, and then the cold; and when they came to the next country they were not welcome.

That country did not have a king, but a sultan. He sent for the King to ask why he had come. He heard the story of the wells, how they were dry, and how something came out of them at night and ate the people.

"All the people are afraid to stay in their own land," said the King, "with the drought, and Nebuchendrie."

"I shall send someone to see," said the Sultan. "It is all one thing: Nebuchendrie."

He called for his eldest Prince, Ahmed, who was a soldier. "I will go," said Ahmed. "I will conquer the country for you and bring back all the people. You will be a great emperor, father."

Some soldiers are fairly stupid. The Sultan explained that the people were here already and that he wanted them to go back, and Ahmed was to deal with the wells, and see about the creature that came out of them.

"Left, right," said Ahmed, not listening very much.

He lefted and he righted with an army across the mountains, night and day, until he reached the desert on the other side. It used to be the thousand melon gardens but was now dry and dusty. Here the brave soldier and his army marched, stopped at a well, found no water, marched back, and not being used to it at all, they died beside the road.

"So much for left, right, left, right, all my life," said Ahmed. "This is not a proper coun-try for soldiers."

Ahmed did not get back home.

The Sultan sent his next son, Fazir.

"I don't see any problems," said Fazir. "Nasty

things in wells, is it? Simple. I'll dig some more wells; I don't know why they didn't think of it themselves. And I'll put poison down the old ones, and that'll take care of the nasty black creeping creatures, these Nebuchendries. I should be home in a couple of weeks. I don't think it will take long."

Fazir went by ship. He had no intention of walking over the mountains. He landed with his men, who were scientists, not soldiers. Some went to poison wells; some went to dig them. Fazir went about helping them, and putting flags by the poisoned wells so that no one would make a mistake.

In the night Nebuchendrie came out of the wells and moved the flags about.

In the morning Fazir and his men drank poisoned water. At the seashore their ship floated away and went back home empty.

The Sultan had one more son, Niris. He was a simple man, not interested in being a soldier, or scientist, or even in being sultan one day. He was a farmer, and was happy behind a plough.

"I will go to look," he said to the Sultan. "But what can a farmer do, if the king of the country cannot do it better?"

"Do your best," said the Sultan. "We must send these people back soon."

So Niris was the Prince who came riding over the mountains. He was not looking very princely. He came on his old cart-horse, Dobbin, and he wore his daytime hat and his farming trousers. He brought with him what he had: a spade, a sickle, a plough-share, a scythe, a pitchfork, a rake, a drink of water, a bun; behind him walked his cow dog, and in his pocket was his gully-knife.

He came rattling down into the desert, and stopped at the first well. He tied Dobbin to a tree, and sat down to see what happened. He was used to waiting to see what came out of the ground.

Nebuchendrie came out. Nebuchendrie came out of the well at nightfall, and looked around.

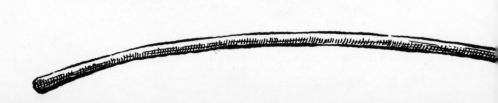

Nebuchendrie licked up the dog, Nebuchendrie gulped down poor Dobbin. Niris kept very still, and saw Nebuchendrie go down the well again.

In the morning Niris took his spade and tied it to his arm. He took his sickle and tied it to his hat. He took his plough-share and tied it to his back. He took his scythe and tied it to his shoulder. He took his pitchfork and tied it to his leg. He took his rake and tied it to his foot. He waited until night came.

At night Nebuchendrie came out of the well, sniffed once, sniffed twice, and a third time, and began to swallow him.

It was not easy to swallow Niris with all his farming tools strapped to him. And Niris took out his gully-knife and fought back.

But Nebuchendrie did not give up. Nebuchendrie bit and bit, although it hurt.

Niris fought, but he could not help being dragged to the edge of the well; he could not help being taken down it. But all the way he stabbed and jabbed; and Nebuchendrie could not swallow him, because he was so prickly and uncomfortable. But Nebuchendrie tried.

Then they were both in the bottom of the well, underground and in the dark.

Niris groaned at the hard work he had to do, far worse than ploughing or haytime; and Nebuchendrie squealed at this sharp mouthful.

Then all at once Nebuchendrie stopped the fight, and went back into a corner. And a little crooked ugly man came to talk to Niris.

"I will give you treasure if you will go away," he said. "I am the master of Nebuchendrie, as I said I would be, and you will kill her if you go on, and I shall be master of no one."

"I do not care for you," said Niris. "Stand aside. I've started this furrow, and I'll finish it."

"But I am master here," said the little old man. "My name is Rianch, and when the Princess was born I took the place of her nurse, and made myself the master, first of her, and now of the kingdom."

"Who gave you the kingdom?" said Niris.

"She is the King's daughter," said Rianch.

"I have heard enough of this tale," said Niris. "You are a weed. I pull you out of the ground. If you want a kingdom I will give you one." And he

whirled Rianch round by one leg, and hurled him out of the well into the air, and out of the air into the sky, as far as the moon, where he can still be seen, king of the kingdom of nothing.

When Niris had done that he turned to finish off Nebuchendrie. But the great black thing like a serpent was no longer there. Instead, there was a very pretty black girl, rubbing her head.

"It no longer aches," she said. "And I no longer need to eat all I see, or drink all the wells dry. That was the spell Rianch put upon me when I was a little girl without a name and I could be changed to that creature."

"So what will you do?" asked Niris. And he lent her his shirt, because she had nothing to wear.

"First I shall free all that I have caught and eaten, because they are all under the ground with me. Take me out of the well, and you will see them come after me, out of every well in the kingdom."

All the creatures, all the people she had eaten, all that died of drought, came alive; Ahmed, Fazir, Dobbin, the dog, all were alive again. And water flowed in the wells.

"Thank you, Nebuchendrie," they all said.

"I will keep that name," said Nebuchendrie. But now she was hungry and thirsty for her own land only. She had never wanted to eat people, drink all the water, or live under the ground.

She and Niris clattered home on Dobbin to the Sultan. All the people of the dry country came back two by two over the mountains to their old villages. The rivers ran, the lakes filled, the cisterns overflowed, and the wells no more ran dry.

Niris and Nebuchendrie were married not long afterwards and followed them.

Before long the King said, "I am tired of the cares

of a thousand cows and a thousand sheep. My daughter may milk and shear them."

And the Queen said, "I am weary of a thousand fields and a thousand melon gardens. Let my daughter reap and water them."

And they both retired. Niris became King, Nebuchendrie Queen, and they stayed at home to farm, to bring up their princes and princesses themselves.

And the people who had been eaten by the Queen were proud of it.

"Some tasted better than others," she says privately to Niris. "But I do not know which was which. I know that you were worst, and I am glad of it."

And for ever we know whose shape we see on the moon.